The Adventures of Sherlock Holmes

Treasury of Illustrated Classics™

The Adventures of Sherlock Holmes

by
Sir Arthur Conan Doyle

Adapted by
Kathy Wilmore

Illustrated by
Ned Butterfield

Modern Publishing
A Division of Unisystems, Inc.
New York, New York 10022

Series UPC: 39340

Cover art by Brian Bartle

Contents

MR. SHERLOCK HOLMES

I

In 1878, I graduated from the University of London as a doctor of medicine. I then became a surgeon, and joined the army as an assistant surgeon. I was sent to a unit stationed in India. War had broken out with Afghanistan by the time I got there. My unit was deep in enemy country, so I had plenty of work to do.

Misfortune struck quickly. I was hit by an enemy bullet, and I would have died if my aide hadn't carried me to safety. For months, I lay in a hospital with a terrible fever that almost killed me. I finally recovered, but I was so weak and thin that the army sent me back to England to regain my health.

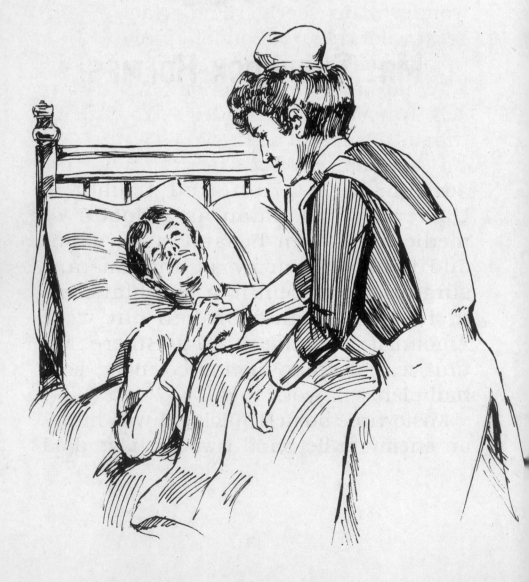

I had no friends or family in London, so I moved into a hotel. It was an expensive way to live, so I decided to look for cheaper lodgings.

The very day I decided this, I ran into Stamford, an old schoolmate. It was wonderful to see a friendly face in the great wilderness of London! I invited him to join me for lunch.

"What have you been doing with yourself, Watson?" he asked me. "You are as thin as a rail and as brown as a nut."

I gave him a short sketch of my army adventures.

"Poor devil!" he said. "What are you up to now?"

"Looking for lodgings," I answered. "But how do you find comfortable rooms at a reasonable price?"

"That's strange," said Stamford. "You're the second man today to say that to me."

"Who was the first?"

"A fellow who studies at the chemical

laboratory at the hospital where I work. He was complaining this morning about not having someone to share a nice apartment that he'd found but can't afford on his own."

"If he wants someone to share it with, I am the very man for him!" I cried.

Stamford gave me a strange look. "You don't know Sherlock Holmes yet," he said. "Perhaps you wouldn't like him."

"Why? What's wrong with him?"

"I didn't say there was anything wrong

with him. He's a little strange, but seems to be a good enough fellow."

"Is he a medical student?" I asked.

"Not exactly," said Stamford. "I don't know what he's studying. He knows a lot about anatomy and chemistry, though, and his knowledge often astonishes the professors."

"Well, I'd like to judge for myself," I said. "May I meet this friend of yours?"

"He'll be at the lab," said Stamford. "Some weeks, he works there from

morning until night. We can go there after we have our lunch."

That settled, we talked of other things, enjoying our meal.

II

As we headed for the lab after lunch, Stamford warned me: "Don't blame me if you don't get along with him," he said. "I know nothing of him other than what I've told you. Remember, this is *your* idea."

"If we don't get along, I can move out," I said. "But Stamford, you seem to have some reason for being worried. Is this fellow bad-tempered, or what?"

"Holmes is a little too scientific for my tastes—almost cold-blooded," Stamford replied. "I can imagine him slipping some chemical into a friend's food just to see how it works on the human body. To be fair, though, I think that he'd take it himself just as readily. He has a passion for exact knowledge."

"That's fine with me," I quickly replied.

"Yes, but he carries it a bit far. Here we are." As he spoke, we entered the hospital's laboratory.

The room was littered with countless bottles, test tubes, and Bunsen burners. There was only one student in sight, bending over a table, absorbed in his work. At the sound of our footsteps, he cried, "I've found it! I've found it!" and ran toward us with a test tube in his hand. "I've found a substance that is activated by blood and nothing else." If he had discovered a gold mine, he couldn't have looked more delighted.

"Dr. James Watson, meet Mr. Sherlock Holmes," said Stamford.

"How are you?" said Holmes, gripping my hand with surprising strength. "You have been in Afghanistan, I see."

"How did you know that?" I asked in astonishment.

"Never mind," said he, chuckling to himself. "The question now is about blood. Surely you see the importance of my discovery?"

"It's interesting," I said, "but—"

"Why, it is the most practical medico-

legal discovery in years! It gives us a fool-proof test for blood stains. Come here!" He pulled me over to the table where he'd been working. "Let's have some fresh blood." He poked a needle into his finger-tip and squeezed out a drop of blood. "I'll add this small amount of blood to a liter of water. You can't even see it—it looks like pure water. But watch!" He threw a few white crystals into the glass jar, then added a few drops of a clear fluid. In an instant, the mixture turned a deep reddish brown, and a brownish dust sifted to the bottom of the jar.

"Ha!" he cried, clapping his hands. "Proof of the presence of blood! It works no matter how old the blood is, or how little there is. If this test had been invented sooner, countless guilty men now walking about free would long ago have paid for their crimes!"

"Indeed," I murmured.

"Think how many criminal cases hang on that one point! A man is suspected of a crime, perhaps months after it occurred. His clothes are found to have stains on them. But are they blood stains or mud stains? Rust or fruit stains? There was no reliable test. Now, however, we have the Sherlock Holmes test!"

His eyes gleamed with pride, and he put his hand over his heart and bowed, as if to a cheering crowd.

"Congratulations," I said.

"We came here on business," Stamford told Holmes. "My friend here is looking for lodgings, and since you were complaining that you couldn't get anyone to share with you, I thought that I should bring you two together."

Sherlock Holmes seemed delighted at the idea of sharing his rooms with me. "I have my eye on a place on Baker Street," he said. "I usually have chemicals about. Will that annoy you?"

"Not at all," I said.

"Let me see—what are my other shortcomings? I get down in the dumps at times, and don't open my mouth for days on end. Just leave me alone when I do that, and I'll be all right in a while. What do *you* have to confess?"

I laughed at this questioning. "Well, I don't like a lot of noise," I said, "because my nerves are easily shaken. I get up at all sorts of hours, and I'm extremely lazy."

"Do you count violin playing as noise?" he asked anxiously.

"Not if it's well played," I answered. "A well-played violin is a treat for the gods. A badly played one—"

"Oh, that's all right," he cried, with a merry laugh. "Meet me here tomorrow at noon. We'll settle everything then."

"All right—noon exactly," I said, shaking his hand.

Stamford and I left Holmes working among his chemicals, and walked back toward my hotel.

"By the way," I asked, stopping suddenly. "How on earth did he know that I've just come from Afghanistan?"

Stamford smiled an odd little smile. "That's just his little peculiarity," he said. "A lot of people want to know how he finds things out."

"Oh, a mystery, is it?" I cried, rubbing my hands. "This is very interesting. Thank you for bringing us together. 'The proper study of mankind is man,' you know."

"Well, study him then," said Stamford. "You'll find him a knotty problem, though. I'll bet he learns a lot more about you than you learn about him!"

CASE #1

THE ADVENTURE OF THE SPECKLED BAND

I

I woke one morning to find Sherlock Holmes standing, fully dressed, by the side of my bed. Usually, he was a late riser, but it was only 7:15. I blinked at him in surprise.

"Sorry to wake you early, Watson," Holmes said, "but Mrs. Hudson, our landlady, says that a very agitated young lady insists on seeing me. She's waiting in the sitting room. When young ladies wander about London at this hour of the morning and rouse sleepy people from their beds, something urgent must be at hand. This may be an interesting case. Would you like to be in on it from the beginning?"

"My dear fellow, I wouldn't miss it for anything!" I replied. I threw on my clothes, then followed my friend to the sitting room. A woman dressed in black, with a heavy veil over her face, was sitting by the window. She stood up as we entered.

"Good morning, ma'am," said Holmes cheerfully. "My name is Sherlock

Holmes. This is my friend and associate, Dr. Watson. You may speak as freely before him as you would to me. Please, sit by the fire—I see that you are shivering."

"It's not from the cold," said the woman, though she did move closer to the fire. "It's from fear, Mr. Holmes. It's from terror."

She raised her veil as she spoke. Her face was pale and pinched-looking, with restless, frightened eyes like those of a trapped animal. She looked young, but

her hair was streaked with gray. Holmes gave her one of his quick but thorough glances, taking everything in.

"Have no fear," he said gently. "We'll soon set matters right. You came in by train this morning, I see."

"You know me?" she asked in surprise.

"No," said Holmes. "But I see the second half of a return train ticket stuck in your left glove. You must have started early. You had to ride a while in a small carriage along country roads before reaching the station."

The woman stared at my friend in awe.

"There's no mystery, dear lady," he said with a smile. "The left sleeve of your jacket is spattered with mud in no less than seven places. The marks are fresh. Only a small carriage would throw up mud that way, and then only when you're sitting next to the driver."

"You're right!" she said. "I left home before six this morning, reached the Leatherhead station at twenty past, and

came in to London by the first train. I've heard of you from a friend, Mrs. Farintosh, who told me how you helped her in her hour of need. Can you help me in mine? I can't afford to pay you now, but in a month I'll be married. I will then have control of the money my mother left me in her will. I could pay you then."

"Madam, I'll be happy to give your case the same care that I gave your friend's," said Holmes. "As for money, an interesting case is its own reward. You may pay any expenses that come up, if and when you wish. But now, please tell us everything about what's troubling you."

II

"My name is Helen Stoner," said our visitor. "I live with my stepfather, who is the last survivor of one of the oldest families in England, the Roylott family of Stoke Moran. Perhaps you have heard of my stepfather's family?"

Holmes nodded. "I'm familiar with that name."

"The family was once one of the richest in England. But several recent Roylotts were lazy, wasteful men who gambled away most of the fortune and land. All that's left is a few acres of ground and a 200-year-old mansion. My stepfather couldn't count on the estate for his livelihood, so he borrowed money and went to medical school. Then he moved to India and did very well there. He'd always had an awful temper, however, and in a fit of rage he beat one of his servants to death. It was a terrible scandal. He served a long prison sentence. Afterward, he returned to England a bitter man.

"While still in India, Dr. Roylott met and married my mother, the young widow of Major-General Stoner. My twin sister, Julia, and I were two years old then. Our mother had quite a fortune—at least £1,000 a year. Her will left all her money in Dr. Roylott's control. The only exception was that a certain amount was to go to my sister and me when we married.

"Eight years ago, shortly after we moved to England, Mother was killed in a railway accident. Dr. Roylott moved us to his family's estate at Stoke Moran. The money Mother had left him was enough for us all to live there comfortably. But instead of making friends in the town, our stepfather shut himself in the house. Whenever he came out, he got into fierce

quarrels with everyone he met. People fled when they saw him coming! The only people he will allow near him now is a band of wandering gypsies, which camps on the estate's grounds. He spends most of his time with the wild animals he had sent here from India. He lets a cheetah and a baboon roam free, which further terrifies the townsfolk.

"My sister and I had no friends. After all, who'd want to visit us? Few servants dared to work there, either, so we usually did the housework ourselves. Julia was just thirty when she died, but already her hair was turning gray, just as mine is."

"Your sister is dead?" asked Holmes.

"Yes," said Miss Stoner. "She died two years ago. I'm here, Mr. Holmes, because I'm afraid that the same thing is about to happen to me!"

"Go on," said Holmes.

"The only pleasure Julia and I had was when we were allowed to visit Miss

Honoria Westphail, our mother's sister. On our visit two Christmases ago, Julia met a young marine, and they became engaged. Our stepfather said nothing against the marriage, but just two weeks before the wedding, a dreadful event took my dear sister's life."

Holmes had been leaning back in his chair with his eyes closed. He half-opened them now to glance at Miss Stoner. "Give me every detail," he said.

"We live in one wing of the old house.

The other has been shut up, since we don't need the rooms. The sitting rooms are in the center of the building, and the bedrooms are in our wing, all on the ground floor. The first bedroom is Dr. Roylott's, the second was Julia's, the third is mine—all in a row. There are no doors between them, but all open into the same hallway. All three rooms have windows facing the lawn. You understand?"

"Perfectly," Holmes replied.

"On that fatal night, Dr. Roylott went

to his room early, but we knew that he hadn't gone to bed, since my sister could smell the strong Indian tobacco he smokes in his pipe. It bothered her, so she came to my room for a while, to talk about her wedding plans. As she left at eleven o'clock, she paused at the door.

" 'Tell me, Helen,' she said, 'have you ever heard anyone whistle in the dead of the night?'

" 'Never,' I said. 'Why?'

" 'The last few nights, I've heard a low whistle about three in the morning. It wakes me up. I can't tell where it comes from.'

" 'I haven't heard it,' I said, 'but it must be the gypsies, out on the lawn.'

" 'I suppose so,' she said. 'Well, it's not important. Good night.' She smiled at me, shut my door, and a few moments later I heard her key turn in the lock."

"Key?" said Holmes. "Did you and your sister usually lock yourselves in?"

"Always! We never felt safe from the

cheetah and baboon unless we locked our doors at night."

"Quite so. Please continue."

"I couldn't sleep. The wind was howling, rain was slashing at the windows, and I couldn't shake a feeling of doom. Suddenly, I heard a terrified woman's scream. It was my sister's voice! I rushed into the hallway. Just then, I heard a low whistle. Moments later, I heard a clanging sound, as of falling metal. When I reached Julia's door, the key turned in the lock and the door swung open. My sister appeared in the doorway, her face white with terror and her body swaying. I threw my arms around her, but she fell to the ground, writhing as if in terrible pain. As I bent over her, she shrieked and said, 'Oh, my God! Helen! It was the band! The speckled band!' She pointed toward the doctor's room. I ran for his door, calling out for help, and met him in the hallway, rushing toward us. By the time he reached Julia's side, she was

unconscious. He tried to revive her, but she died."

"Are you sure about this whistle and metallic sound?" asked Holmes.

"Yes," said Miss Stoner. "I'm sure."

"Was your sister dressed?"

"No, she was in her nightgown. In her right hand was a burned-out match, and in her left hand she held a matchbox."

"So she had struck a light and looked about her," said Holmes. "That's very important. Did the police investigate?"

"Yes, thoroughly—especially since Dr. Roylott is well-known as a violent man. But they never found a clear cause of death. Julia's door had been locked from the inside, and her windows were blocked by shutters with iron bars that are locked shut every night. The chimney is barred, too. The walls are solid all around; so is the floor. My sister was alone when terror struck, and there were no bruises or other marks of violence on her."

"What about poison?" asked Holmes.

"The doctors examined her for it, but found no evidence of it."

"What do *you* think she died of?"

"Pure fear and nervous shock," said Miss Stoner, "but I have no idea of what frightened her."

"What do you suppose she meant by 'the speckled band'?"

"Sometimes I think that she was just babbling with terror. Other times I think she meant a band of people, such as the gypsies. Some gypsies wear dotted bandannas on their heads."

Holmes shook his head, looking dissatisfied. "That was two years ago. Why come to me now?"

"A month ago, a dear friend of many years, Mr. Percy Armitage, asked me to marry him. My stepfather had no objections, and we are to be married this spring. Two days ago, repairmen began working on the west wing of the house, starting at my end. I've had to move from my room to Julia's. Last night, I lay in her bed, thinking about what had happened to her. Imagine my terror when I heard, in the deep of night, a low whistle! I sprang up and lit the lamp, but saw nothing. I got dressed and, as soon as it was daylight, slipped out of

the house and ran to town, where I hired a carriage to take me to the train. I came straight here."

"That was wise," said Holmes. "We haven't a moment to lose. If we went to Stoke Moran today, could we examine the rooms without your stepfather knowing?"

"Yes, he has business in town today," said Miss Stoner. "He won't be back until evening."

"Excellent! Expect us early in the afternoon. Will you be all right till then?"

"Oh, yes! Talking to you has lightened my heart. I look forward to seeing you again this afternoon." She dropped her veil back over her face and left us.

III

"What do you make of all this, Watson?" asked my friend.

"It seems a sinister business. If the lady is correct about the walls and floors being solid, and the door, window, and chimney impassable, then her sister had to be alone when she met her end," I replied.

"What about those whistles, and the lady's strange dying words?" said Holmes.

"I have no idea."

"The answer lies in the details. That's why we're going to Stoke Moran. I must see the place for myself. Wait! What's this?" Holmes asked.

Our door had crashed open and a huge man filled the doorway. His face was wrinkled by long hours in the sun, and his sharp nose and deep-set, flashing eyes gave him the look of a fierce hawk.

"Which of you is Holmes?" the giant demanded.

"I am," said my friend quietly. "Who are you?"

"Dr. Grimesby Roylott of Stoke Moran," said the giant.

"Indeed," said Holmes. "Please, Dr. Roylott, take a seat."

"No! My stepdaughter was here. What has she been telling you?"

"It's a little cold for this time of year," said Holmes calmly.

"What has she told you?" screamed Dr. Roylott.

"I've heard that the crocuses are blooming quite well, however," continued Holmes, as if he hadn't noticed the man's rage.

"You think you can ignore me?" the man shouted. "I've heard of you, Holmes! You're a meddler, a busybody."

Holmes chuckled. "Your conversation is most entertaining, Doctor," he said. "When you go out, please shut the door—there's a draft."

"I'll go when I'm ready! I followed Miss Stoner here, and I'm telling you right now: Stay out of our business. I'm a dangerous man to cross. Watch this!" He stepped over to the fireplace, picked up the steel poker, and bent it into a curve with his huge hands. "Keep away!" He threw down the twisted poker and stormed out.

"I'm nowhere near his size," said Holmes, laughing. "But if he'd stayed a little longer, I might have shown him that I'm his match in strength of grip." He picked up the poker and, with a sudden effort, straightened it out again.

IV

We took an early afternoon train to Leatherhead. On the way, Holmes told me how he had spent the rest of his morning tracking down a copy of Mrs. Roylott's will. She had £1,110 when she died; only about £750 were left. Each daughter, if she married, could claim £250. If both got married, Dr. Roylott would have a big drop in his income.

When we reached Stoke Moran, Miss Stoner hurried to greet us.

"We've had the pleasure of meeting your stepfather," said Holmes. He told her what had happened after she left us. The poor lady turned pale with fright.

"Good heavens!" she cried. "What will he do to me when he returns?"

"Don't worry," said Holmes. "We won't let any harm come to you. For now, we have work to do. Let me see those rooms."

The old building was made of stone. There was a high central section with two curving wings, like the claws of a crab, on each side. In one wing, the windows were broken and blocked with wooden boards and the roof looked half caved in. The other wing looked much nicer, with blinds on the windows and smoke curling up from the chimneys.

Scaffolding at the end showed where repairs were being made, but no workers were in sight. Holmes walked up and down the lawn in front of this wing, carefully examining the windows.

"This," he said, pointing, "is your room, the middle one your sister's, and the one next to the main building is Dr. Roylott's?"

"Yes," said Miss Stoner. "But I'm sleeping in the middle room now."

"So I understand," said Holmes. "By the way, I see no urgent need for repairs at that end of the wall."

"Neither do I," said she. "I think it's an excuse to force me from my room."

"Ah," said Holmes. "Are there windows in the hallway opposite these rooms?"

"Yes, but they're too small for anyone to climb through."

"You both locked your doors at night, so no one could have entered from that side, anyway," said Holmes. "Now, please go to the middle room and bar the shutters."

She did so. Holmes tried to force the shutters open from the outside, but could not. He took out his magnifying glass and studied the hinges.

"All solid," he said. "Nothing could come in this way. Let's look inside."

The room where Miss Stoner was now sleeping—once her sister's—seemed unremarkable. It was a small room with a low ceiling and a large fireplace, like those in many country houses. There was a chest of drawers in one corner, a narrow bed in another corner, and a small table just left of the window. Two chairs and a carpet in the middle of the floor were the room's only other furnishings. Holmes pulled up a chair and sat, silently gazing around the room.

"Where is the bell?" he asked, pointing to a thick bell-pull rope hanging close to the bed—so close that its tasseled end touched the edge of the pillow.

"In the housekeeper's room. The pull was put in a couple of years ago."

"Your sister asked for it?"

"No, she never used it."

"It seems unnecessary to put such a nice bell-pull there, then," said Holmes. "Excuse me a moment." He got out his magnifying glass again and crawled about on his hands and knees, examining every inch of the floor and walls. Then he went to the bell-pull and stared at it. Finally, he grabbed it and tugged.

"It's a fake," he said. "It's not attached to a wire—just to a hook up near that little air vent."

"How absurd!" said Miss Stoner. "I never noticed that before."

"Very strange," said Holmes. "There are some very curious things about this room. First, why would the builder put an air vent in a wall that goes to another room, when he could put it in an outside wall?"

"That vent is new, too. It was put in around the same time as the bell rope," said Miss Stoner.

"Interesting changes," said Holmes. "Bell-pulls with no bells, vents that don't ventilate. Now, let's go see what your stepfather's room looks like."

Dr. Roylott's room was larger than his stepdaughter's, but as plainly furnished: a small bed, a wooden shelf full of books, an armchair by the bed, a plain wooden chair against the wall, a round table, and a large iron safe. Holmes walked around the room, examining everything with keen interest.

"What's in here?" he asked, tapping the safe.

"Only papers," said Miss Stoner. "I saw inside it once, years ago."

"There wasn't a cat in it?" Holmes asked her.

"What a strange idea!" said the lady. "No. We don't have a cat. Only the cheetah and the baboon."

"Well, a cheetah is just a big cat," said my friend, "but this little saucer of milk on the floor wouldn't satisfy it." He studied the chair, especially its seat. Then something else caught his eye—a small

dog's leash hanging on a corner of the bedpost. It was curled up and tied with a loop at one end.

"What do you make of that, Watson?" said Holmes.

"It's a common dog's leash," I said. "But I don't see why it's tied like that."

"Then it's not so common, is it? And there's no dog. Ah, me! It's a wicked world. Miss Stoner, you must listen carefully and do exactly as I say."

"I will," she said.

"When your stepfather comes back, pretend that you have a headache and

stay in your sister's room. We'll be watching from outside. When you hear him turn in for the night, open the shutters, unlock the window, and put a lamp there to signal us. Then lock yourself in your old room. Watson and I will spend the night in your sister's room and investigate this odd noise."

"Do you know what happened to my sister?" she asked.

"I think so, but I need proof," Holmes told her. "Be brave and follow my instructions. All will be well."

V

Holmes and I went a safe distance and watched the house. "You must have seen more than I did, Holmes," I said while we waited.

"No, we saw the same things. I just deduced more."

"I didn't see anything strange but the bell rope."

"What about the vent?" Holmes asked.

"Lots of houses have them. Besides, it's so small, a rat could hardly get through. It can't mean much."

"Ah, but it does," said my friend. "It's all in the timing: A vent is put in, a cord is hung, and a lady who sleeps in the bed nearby dies. And didn't you notice that the bed had been clamped to the floor? The lady couldn't have moved it if she'd wanted to. It would always be that close to the bell-pull and vent."

"That *is* strange!" I admitted.

We kept our watch. At about eleven o'clock, we saw a lamp shine out.

"Our signal!" said Holmes. "We must be very quiet, Watson, and never let down our guard. Our lives and the lady's depend on it!"

We climbed in through the window. Holmes sat on the bed and laid his cane beside him, along with a box of matches and a candlestick. I sat in the chair, my army revolver by my hand.

Hours passed. We lit no light and spoke

no word—just sat, alert to every sound. The village clock struck twelve, then one, two, and three. Just past three, we heard a rustle of movement in the doctor's room. Some minutes later, we heard a strange sound, like the small hiss of steam escaping from a kettle. Holmes leaped to his feet, lit the candles, then began lashing furiously at the bell-pull with this cane!

"See it, Watson?" he yelled loudly. "Do you see it?"

I saw nothing. As Holmes lashed and yelled, however, we heard a low whistle. My friend's face was deadly pale and full of horror, but he stopped swinging the cane and stared up at the vent. Suddenly, the night was ripped by the most horrible scream I have ever heard. It grew louder and louder, then faded into an echo.

"It's all over," said my friend. "Let's go to the doctor's room."

Holmes lit the lamp and we went to the hall, where he knocked twice on Dr. Roylott's door. No answer. He turned the knob and we entered.

In the flickering candlelight, we saw a horrible scene. The door of the safe stood open. Beside it sat Dr. Grimesby Roylott in a long robe and slippers. Across his lap was the odd leash we had seen earlier. His head was thrown back and his face was frozen into a dreadful stare. Tight around his brow was an odd yellow band, with brownish speckles.

"The band!" whispered Holmes. "The speckled band!"

Just then, the band moved, twisting up to reveal itself as a huge serpent.

"Stand back!" cried Holmes. "That's a swamp adder, the deadliest snake in India. Its bite kills within seconds!" He snatched up the leash, slipped its loop around the adder's head, and tossed it into the safe, slamming the door shut. It clanged with the sound of falling metal, as Miss Stoner had described. "Let's get Miss Stoner to a safe place," said Holmes. "Then we'll call in the police."

VI

We took the terrified young woman to her aunt's house. The police investigated and decided that the doctor had died while playing with a dangerous pet. Holmes knew otherwise, but said nothing. He filled me in as we rode the train back to London.

"I almost got it wrong," he said.

"That's why it's so important to gather enough data! I was almost misled by Miss Stoner's talk of gypsies, cheetahs, and baboons. I knew that there was a vent, since Miss Stoner had said that her sister could smell the doctor's pipe smoke. But it didn't mean much until I saw the room, with its bell-pull, vent, and clamped bed. That's when the idea of a snake came to me. A snake could fit through that vent and go down that rope. There was no guarantee that it would bite the lady the first time, of course, so the doctor trained it to return when he whistled, rewarding it with a saucer of milk. He tried several times before it bit Miss Julia, and he was prepared to keep trying until it got Miss Helen. The police doctor missed the tiny bite marks on Miss Julia's body—easy to do.

"Examining Dr. Roylott's room told me more. By studying his chair, which was close to the vent, I could tell that he'd been standing on it. The leash and the saucer of milk confirmed my idea of a snake, and I realized that the clang Miss Stoner had heard was her stepfather slamming the safe door on his dangerous pet. Tonight, when I heard the creature's hiss, as I'm sure you did, I knew it was coming. I instantly lit the candles and attacked the beast. It slithered back up the rope at once."

"And back through the vent," I said.

"Yes," said my friend. "No doubt it was enraged by my attack, and turned on its owner. Therefore, I am at least indirectly responsible for Dr. Grimesby Roylott's death—but I cannot say that my conscience is too bothered about it. Miss Stoner is safe, and she has a chance for happiness at last!"

THE RED-HEADED LEAGUE

I

One day I arrived at Baker Street to find my friend in deep conversation with a stout, red-faced, elderly gentleman with fiery red hair.

"You couldn't have come at a better time, Watson," said Holmes. He turned to his visitor. "Mr. Wilson, this gentleman has helped me in many of my most successful cases. I'm sure he'll be useful in your case, too."

Holmes waved me to a seat and took

his own, putting his fingertips together to get ready for thinking. "You may remember me saying, Watson, that real life offers far more strange and interesting combinations than anything born of the imagination."

"An idea that I told you I find hard to believe," I said.

"You did, but you'll soon come around to my point of view. Mr. Jabez Wilson here has a story that may be the oddest I've heard in some time. Will you be so kind, Mr. Wilson, as to begin your story again, for Dr. Watson's benefit?"

Holmes's client puffed out his chest with pride and pulled a dirty, wrinkled newspaper from his coat pocket. I tried to study him the way Holmes would, but I didn't discover much. Wilson looked like an everyday sort of working man—pudgy, stuffy, and slow. He wore baggy trousers, a dull vest with a gold watch chain and a squared coin dangling from it, and a not-very-clean

jacket. The only remarkable thing about him was his blazing red hair and the unhappy look on his face.

Holmes noticed what I was doing, and smiled. "Beyond the obvious fact that Mr. Wilson has at some time done manual labor, has been in China, and has done a lot of writing lately, I can deduce nothing else."

Wilson jolted upright and stared at my friend in astonishment.

"How did you know that?" he asked.

"It's true that I once did manual labor—I started as a ship's carpenter!"

"Your right hand is a whole glove size larger than your left," said Holmes. "You have worked with it, so its muscles are more developed."

"And the writing?"

"Your right cuff is shiny for five inches—it's been rubbing on the desk as you write. Your left elbow is shiny, too, where you rest it on the desk."

"That's true, too! But China?"

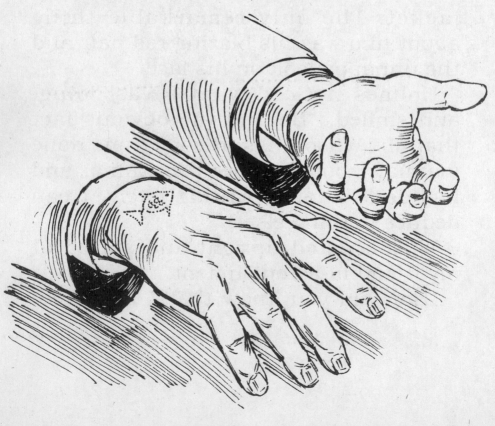

"The fish tattooed on your right wrist could only have been done there. I have made a study of tattoo marks. Staining the fish's scales that shade of pink is quite particular to China. I also see a Chinese coin hanging from your watch chain. Nothing could be more simple."

Wilson laughed heartily. "Oh-ho!" he said. "At first I thought that you'd done something clever, but now I see that there was nothing to it, after all."

"I'm beginning to think, Watson," said Holmes, "that it's a mistake to explain. Mr. Wilson, have you found that ad?"

"Yes," he said, handing it to me. I read:

TO THE RED-HEADED LEAGUE:

There is a job now open that entitles a member of the League to a salary of £4 a week for minor tasks. All red-headed men of sound body and mind and above the age of 21 are eligible. Apply in person to Duncan Ross at the League offices, at 7 Pope's Court, Fleet Street.

"This is extraordinary!" I exclaimed after reading it twice.

Holmes chuckled in delight. "It is, isn't it?" said he. "Now let's listen to Mr. Wilson's story. First, Watson, note the paper's date."

"August 27, 1890—that was just two months ago."

"I have a small pawnbroker's business in Coburg Square," said Wilson. "I do all right, but just barely. I can afford only one assistant, and I couldn't afford even him if he hadn't agreed to work for half wages to learn the business."

"What is the name of this obliging youth?" asked Holmes.

"Vincent Spaulding," replied Wilson, "and he's not all that young. I couldn't ask for a smarter assistant. He could make lots more money elsewhere, but why should I put ideas in his head?"

"Indeed," said Holmes. "Your good fortune in such an assistant may be as remarkable as your advertisement."

"Oh, he's not perfect," said Wilson. "He's forever snapping away with his camera, and diving into the basement to develop his pictures. But he's a good worker. I was content with my life—till Spaulding showed me that ad. 'I sure wish,' he said, 'that I was a red-headed man. There's a vacancy on the League of Red-headed Men! It's worth quite a little fortune to the man who gets it.'

"I'd never heard of the League, which amazed Spaulding. He said that I was perfect for it—and could easily earn a couple of hundred a year for almost no work. The League, he told me, was founded by an eccentric American millionaire who wanted to help his fellow redheads succeed in life. He left his enormous fortune to just that purpose. I was tempted, but remarked that millions of men would surely show up.

" 'Not as many as you'd think,' said Spaulding. 'I hear that the hair must be a particular shade of red—like yours, I think. Why not at least give it a try and see what happens?'

"So I did, and Spaulding went with me. Fleet Street was mobbed with men with every shade of red hair imaginable! I was about to give up in despair, but Spaulding wouldn't let me. He pushed and shoved us toward the front of the line, where a man with bright red hair was seated at a table. 'This is Mr. Jabez Wilson,' said Spaulding, 'and he's interested in your vacancy.'

" 'He's perfect for it,' said the man,

hopping from his chair to examine me more closely—almost rudely. Then he grabbed my hair and tugged till I cried out in pain. 'Sorry,' he said, 'but I had to be sure it wasn't a wig, or dyed. You wouldn't believe what some people will try!'

"That man—Duncan Ross—sent everyone else away and gave me the job. I was very pleased, I can tell you. He laid down the rules: The hours were ten to two, which was fine—most of a pawnbroker's work is done in the evenings, and Spaulding said he'd watch the shop for

me. The pay was £4 a week; also fine. All I had to do was stay in the office for those hours. If I left for any reason, I'd be fired immediately. My job was to copy out the *Encyclopedia Britannica*, starting with Volume I. I started the very next day. I have been working away at it all these eight weeks. I'd almost finished the A's and was looking forward to starting the B's. Then, suddenly, the whole business came to an end—this morning! I arrived at work to find this note pinned to the door." He held up a piece of white cardboard, on which the following message had been written:

THE RED-HEADED LEAGUE
IS DISSOLVED.
OCTOBER 9, 1890.

"I went to the landlord," Wilson continued, "and asked where I might find my employer, Mr. Duncan Ross. But he'd never heard of Ross—or the League.

THE RED-HEADED
LEAGUE
IS DISSOLVED
OCTOBER 9 1890

When I described Ross, he said, 'Oh, that's William Morris, a lawyer. He was only using the space temporarily, while his office was being redecorated. Here's his address.' I hurried over there, but it was a factory, not legal offices, and no one there had ever heard of Ross, Morris, or anyone fitting his description. I hate to lose that extra cash, Mr. Holmes. Can you help me?"

"I wouldn't miss this case for anything in the world," said Holmes. "Please answer a few questions for me. How long had Spaulding worked for you when he showed you the ad?"

"About a month."

"How did you find him?"

"He answered an ad I'd put out."

"Was he the only applicant?"

"No, there were dozens."

"Why did you pick him?"

"Because he would work cheap."

"What does he look like?"

"Small, stout, no hair on his face,

though he's at least 30. He has a splash of white acid on his forehead."

Holmes sat up in excitement. "I thought so! Is he still working for you?"

"Certainly," said Wilson.

"Thank you," said Holmes. "That will do. Today is Saturday. We should have this settled before Monday."

Wilson shook our hands and left.

II

"A truly mysterious business, Holmes!" said I.

"Usually," said Holmes, "the more bizarre something seems to be, the less mysterious it really is. It is the commonplace crimes that are hardest to solve, because there is nothing distinctive to latch on to. Come, Watson, let's take a stroll."

We took a walk by Coburg Square. There was Wilson's shop, a few other businesses, and a few small houses— nothing remarkable. Holmes looked up and down, taking in everything. In front of Wilson's shop, he paused and thumped his cane on the sidewalk a few times, then knocked at the door. Out popped the fellow Wilson had described.

"Pardon me," said Holmes. "We're lost. How do we get to . . ."

The young man gave us directions, and we were off.

"Well," I said. "You seem very interested in Wilson's assistant. I guess you wanted a look at him."

"Not him," said Holmes. "The knees of his trousers. I saw what I expected to see. Now, let's see what's around the corner."

The street behind Wilson's shop was far livelier than Coburg Square. Holmes observed every building, and the steady stream of busy people. "There is a newspaper shop, a vegetarian restaurant, a large bank, and a cab station," he said. "I see now that Wilson's problem is not as small and amusing as I thought—it's quite serious. I must go see to some business. Can you help me tonight?"

"Of course! When?"

"Let's meet at Baker Street at ten. And Watson—get out your army pistol. Our lives may depend on it."

III

When I reached Baker Street that night, Holmes was not alone. Peter

Jones, a police detective we know, was there. So was a man introduced to me as Mr. Merryweather.

"Tonight," said Holmes, "Jones will arrest John Clay—murderer, thief, and master forger. For you, Mr. Merryweather, tonight is worth £30,000."

Holmes led us back to the busy street

we had visited that morning. Then Merryweather led us down a dark alley and through several doors and gates, unlocking all, then relocking them behind us. We ended up in a huge cellar, filled with crates.

"You're safe from above," said Holmes, raising his lantern to check the ceiling.

"From below, too," said Merryweather, striking his cane on the floor. "Dear me!" he cried. "It sounds quite hollow!"

"Quiet!" hissed Holmes. "You may have endangered our entire mission! Please go sit on that crate!" He ordered each of us to a shadowy corner to sit in silence. He took the lantern and his large magnifying glass and got down on his knees. He crawled

about, examining the rough stone floor, especially the cracks between the stones. Then he sprang up, looking pleased. "We have at least an hour to wait. They can't start their work until our red-headed friend, Mr. Wilson, goes to bed. Then they will have to work fast in order to get what they're after, then have plenty of time to escape. I'm sure, Watson, that you've guessed where we are by now: In the basement of the bank we saw this afternoon—on the street around the corner from Mr. Wilson's shop!"

I had seen the bank, of course, but it hadn't meant anything to me at the time.

"Mr. Merryweather here," Holmes continued, waving toward our host, "is the director of this bank. He can tell you what our clever friends are after."

"Our French gold!" whispered the bank director. "We had to borrow 30,000 French gold napoleons a few months ago, but never unpacked them. There are 2,000 of those golden coins in this crate I'm sitting on. There are many others like it, as you can see. It's supposed to be a secret that they're here, but we've been warned that the word is out on the criminals' grapevine. Still, until Mr. Holmes came to me today, I had no idea how close danger was!"

For a while, Holmes let us talk in whispers, but then he ordered complete stillness and silence. He darkened the lantern. He also had me take out my army pistol and have it ready. He asked Jones, the police detective, if Wilson's front door—the criminals' only other way out—was being watched. It was.

We sat and waited. The cold, dank air, mixed with the deep darkness and silence, was depressing. My nerves were jangled with excitement, though, making the hour and a half we waited seem far longer than it really was.

I could feel my muscles growing cramped and stiff, and was trying to stretch without making a sound, when suddenly my eye caught a glint of light. It was coming from the stone floor! In moments, it grew from a mere spark to a thin line to a bright burst. Then, from below, a hand appeared and felt the floor around the hole. It disappeared—then there was a sudden grating noise, and a chunk of floor-stone was turned over. Lantern light spilled into the basement's shadows as a head rose from out of the hole in the floor.

A clean-cut, boyish-looking face squinted into the shadows, but didn't see us. It was the fellow Holmes had asked directions of on our walk earlier that day! He pulled himself up through the hole, then turned to whisper, "All clear, Archie!" Up popped another head—one with a shock of bright red hair. "Let's get to work before—"

Just then, Holmes came flying out from his hiding place. "Great Scott! Run for it, Archie!" yelled the first man, as Holmes grabbed his collar. Jones made a grab for Archie, but all he got was a fistful of cloth as the would-be thief's shirt ripped apart in his hands.

The man in Holmes's grip tried to pull out a gun, but Holmes was too fast for him. He slashed his cane down on the villain's hand, and the man's gun flew away. "It's no use, John

Clay!" Holmes told him, mildly. "You are caught at last."

"So I see," said the other man, cool as could be. "But you've lost my friend."

"No," said Holmes. "He'll be met at the door by three policemen."

"Indeed!" said John Clay. "You've done very well, sir."

"So have you," said Holmes. "Your red-headed league idea was quite brilliant."

Jones stepped forward and clapped handcuffs onto Clay's wrists. Clay glared

and straightened his back indignantly. "I beg you not to touch me with your filthy hands!" he told Jones. "And if you must address me, always say 'sir' and 'please.' I have royal blood in my veins."

Jones snickered, then told his prisoner, "All right, sir. Would you please, sir, march upstairs to the cab that will carry Your Highness to the police station?"

"That's better," sniffed Clay. He made a sweeping bow to Holmes, Merryweather, and me, then stalked off with the police detective.

"Mr. Holmes, I don't know how I can ever thank or repay you!" said Merryweather, shaking my friend's hand.

"I have come across John Clay's wicked trail before," said Holmes. "I'm sure that the bank will repay me. But my biggest reward has been catching that villain— and getting the chance to hear Mr. Wilson's remarkable story of the Red-headed League!"

IV

Back home on Baker Street that night, as we rested by the fire, Holmes filled the gaps in my knowledge of the case.

"You see, Watson," he said, "it was perfectly obvious from the start. There could be only one reason for this incredible business—for the ad in the paper, this Red-headed League, the job of copying the encyclopedia. It was to get the not-very-smart Mr. Jabez Wilson out of his shop for several hours each day. As soon as I heard that Wilson's new assistant was willing to work for so little money, I was sure that he had a very strong reason for wanting to be there and nowhere else."

"How did you know?" I asked.

"Wilson has no wife or daughter, so Clay wasn't after love. Wilson isn't rich, so it wasn't money—at least not his. There were no rare, rich objects in Wilson's house or shop. Then Wilson mentioned his assistant's unusual devotion to photography—and always popping down to the basement. The basement! Once I heard Wilson describe his assistant, I knew for sure that we were dealing with one of London's most brilliant and daring criminals."

"You knew Clay?" I asked.

"We've never seen each other, but I know of his wicked deeds, and have been told what he looks like."

"So we took our walk!"

"Correct," said Holmes. "Remember my remark about the knees of the assistant's pants? They were dirty, wrinkled, and

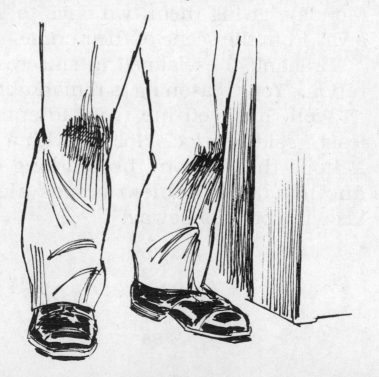

worn thin. He'd been kneeling on them a lot—digging! A tunnel, certainly, but to what? Once we walked around the corner and I saw the bank, I knew. I went at once to the police and the bank director."

"But how did you know that tonight would be the night?" I wanted to know.

"Simple, Watson! They left that sign for Wilson. They didn't have to keep him away anymore—their tunnel was finished. They had to act fast, before their tunnel was discovered or the gold was moved. Saturday would be best: The theft would not be discovered till the bank opened on Monday, giving them two days to get far away from the scene of their crime."

"Brilliant!" I exclaimed in sincere admiration. "Your reasoning is remarkable."

"Well, it saved me from idleness, at least," said Sherlock Holmes with a yawn. "I hope that it won't be too long before another little problem comes along to keep the boredom away!"

A Scandal in Bohemia

I

To Sherlock Holmes, she is always *the* woman. I've seldom heard him mention her by any other name. To him, she is above all other women. It's not that he feels anything like love for Irene Adler. All emotions—love, especially—are alien to his cold, precise, but admirably balanced mind. He is, in my opinion, the most perfect reasoning and observing machine the world has ever seen.

I had not seen much of Holmes lately.

I'd gotten married and moved, while he remained at our lodgings on Baker Street. From time to time I saw reports in the papers of him solving some great crime or other, but that was about it.

One night, I was heading home after tending to a patient when I found myself on Baker Street. I looked up to see Holmes's window brightly lit, and his tall, thin figure pacing the room swiftly, his head sunk on his chest and his hands clasped behind him. I knew all his moods

and habits, and could tell that he was hot on the scent of some new problem. I rang the bell and went up.

"You look happy and healthy, my dear Watson," he said as we settled before the fire. "And in practice again, though you told me that you didn't think you ever would."

"Then how do you know?"

"I see it, I deduce it. I also see that you have been getting yourself very wet lately, and have a clumsy servant girl."

"My dear Holmes, this is too much! In olden days, you'd have been burned at the stake as a witch! I did get wet on Thursday, during a walk in the country, but I've changed my clothes since then. And yes, Mary Jane is hopeless—my wife just fired her. But how do you know these things?"

He chuckled to himself. "Simple, Watson. The leather on the inside of your left shoe is scratched in four parallel cuts. It is obvious that someone

very careless scraped mud from it
recently. So I can see that you've been
out in foul weather, and were not very
well taken care of afterward. As for
your practice, you walked in here
smelling of iodine, with a stethoscope
stored in your hat. I'd be an idiot
indeed not to deduce that you are
practicing medicine again!"

I laughed. "When you explain, it
always seems so ridiculously simple.
But I'm baffled until you point out

each thing and how you've interpreted it! Yet my eyes are as good as yours."

"You *see*, but you don't *observe*," said Holmes. "For instance, you've often climbed the stairs to this apartment."

"Yes, hundreds of times."

"How many steps are there?"

"I don't know."

"Exactly! You haven't observed. By the way, I'm on a new case. My client should be here at any moment. I received a note saying that a man would come at 7:45 p.m.—and not to be surprised that he'll be wearing a mask."

"A mask? How mysterious. What do you suppose that means?" I asked.

"I have no data yet. It is a major mistake to theorize before one has data. It makes you twist facts to fit theories, instead of coming up with theories that fit the facts. We'll have answers soon enough. Here he comes."

There was a loud, authoritative tap, and a man entered. He was more than six-feet, six-inches tall, with powerful arms and chest. He was grandly dressed—obviously a very wealthy man. A black mask covered the upper part of the man's face.

"You received my note?" he asked in a German accent.

"Yes. I am Sherlock Holmes, and this is my friend Dr. Watson. You may trust him as you do me. Please have a seat, and tell us why you are here."

"Call me Count Von Kramm. I must bind you both to absolute secrecy. This is a matter of great importance—it could affect European politics!"

"Of course," said Holmes.

"Excuse the mask. I admit that the name I just gave is not my own."

"I am aware of that," said Holmes, taking a seat and closing his eyes.

This surprised our visitor, who stared.

Holmes opened his eyes and gave the man an impatient look. "If Your Majesty would please tell me why you

are here," he said. "I would be better able to help you."

The man leaped from his chair. "You're right! I'm the king of Bohemia!"

"Indeed," said Holmes. "You hadn't spoken before I was aware of who you are. You are Wilhelm Gottsreich Sigismond von Ornstein, Grand Duke of Cassel-Felstein, and soon to be king of Bohemia."

"Yes, but how—"

"Never mind that now. Why do you seek my help?"

"I'm about to be married, to the daughter of the king of Scandinavia."

"So I've heard."

"The marriage is important to both our countries. Nothing must stop it. But a woman from my past is threatening to do just that."

"Who is she?" asked Holmes.

"Irene Adler, an opera singer. Five years ago, I met her and was fascinated. I wrote her love letters and followed her everywhere. I was young and foolish."

"Was there a secret marriage?" asked Holmes.

"No, nothing like that!" said the king. "But she has the letters, and a photo of us together. She says that she'll show them to my fiancée to make her jealous!"

"Then Your Majesty must pay her whatever she asks."

"She doesn't want money, she wants me. She vowed that I won't marry any woman but her."

"Then have someone take the letters and photograph."

"I tried, but it didn't work. She is going to send them to my fiancée in three days, when our engagement is announced in the newspapers."

"We have plenty of time," said Holmes. "Give me the lady's address, then go back to your hotel. I'll let you know how we progress."

When the king had gone, Holmes turned to me. "Can you come by tomorrow at three, Watson? You may be able to help me."

II

I did as he asked. Holmes was not in when I arrived, but the landlady let me in to wait by the fire. It was nearing four o'clock when a strange, drunken-looking man—a workman with a puffy red face and messy clothes—stumbled in. I leaped up in surprise. As used as I am to my friend's masterful use of disguise, I had to look three times before I

was certain that it was he! He disappeared into his room. He soon returned, looking like his usual self.

"What a day I've had, Watson!" he said, laughing heartily. "I've spent it watching Miss Irene Adler. I hung out with some workers at a stable across the street. It's amazing what they notice and can tell you. I got full biographies on her—and half a dozen other people in the neighborhood I cared nothing about."

"What of Irene Adler?" I asked.

"Oh, all the men are wild about her. They say that she's the daintiest thing under a bonnet. She lives alone, and rarely goes out except to sing. Drives out at five every day and returns at seven. Sees only one male visitor, a Mr. Godfrey Norton, a lawyer. He is dark, handsome, and dashing. As I watched the house, Norton arrived in a cab, in an obvious hurry. He went in, stayed about half an hour—the cab waited—and dashed back out again. 'Drive as fast as you can!' he told the cabbie, and gave two addresses. The second was the church of St. Monica.

"I was about to follow, when Miss Adler's carriage pulled up to her door and she dashed out and climbed in. She *is* a lovely woman, with a face that a man might die for.

" 'The church of St. Monica!' she cried, 'and please hurry!'

"I ran for a cab and told the driver,

'The church of St. Monica, and hurry!' When I got there, the couple were already there and were being married.

"I was afraid that they would slip off on their honeymoon and ruin all my plans. At the church doors, however, they took separate cabs. 'I'll drive out to the park at five as usual,' she told him, and went home. So I went off and made my arrangements."

"Which are?"

"A bite to eat," said Holmes. "But I'd like your help this evening, Doctor."

"I'd be delighted!"

"Good. We must be at Miss Adler's when she returns at seven. Do as I say, nothing more or less, and all will be well."

"Certainly. What?"

"When she arrives, there will be some unpleasantness. Don't interfere, no matter what. I will be taken into the house. Four or five minutes later, you'll find the living room window open. Stand next to it and watch me. When I raise my hand— like this—throw in what I'll give you to throw, then shout, 'Fire!' It'll be a small, harmless device that makes a lot of smoke. After you yell, a lot of other people will join the cry. Walk to the end of the street and wait. I'll meet you there in ten minutes—and by then I'll know where the king's papers are!"

III

Everything went according to plan. As the lady returned from her drive, some men lounging on the corner began fighting. Their flying fists nearly struck her as she stepped from her carriage. Holmes, disguised as a kind-looking churchman, went dashing in to rescue her and was struck senseless.

"Oh! Is the poor man hurt?" asked the lady, obviously worried.

"He's dead!" cried several voices.

"No, he'll be all right!" cried others.

"Bring him in to my couch," said Miss Adler. "He must be seen to!"

Holmes was carried in, and I took my place by the window. I don't know how he felt, but I was ashamed of myself for playing such a trick on such a kind and beautiful creature. Still, at Holmes's signal, I did as he asked. "Fire!" I shouted as smoke poured from the room.

"Fire!" shouted the crowd. I melted away to the corner. Holmes soon joined me there.

"You did very well, Watson," he said.

"The king's letters and photograph are behind a sliding panel hidden in the wall of her bedroom. When smoke filled the house, she ran there to make sure they were all right, and I caught a glimpse of them. She didn't see me. I cried out that it was a false alarm, told her I felt well again, thanked her, and went on my way. In the morning, we'll go there with the king. He can get them himself."

IV

The next morning, I was with Holmes when the king arrived.

"You have them!" he cried, grabbing Holmes excitedly by the shoulders.

"Not yet," said Holmes. "But we'll have them shortly."

As we rode to Miss Adler's in the king's carriage, Holmes told the king all that had happened. "Irene Adler got married yesterday," he said.

"Married! To whom?"

"An English lawyer named Norton."

"But she can't love him! She always said that she loved me."

"Hope that she *does* love him, Your Majesty," said Holmes. "If she does, she doesn't love you anymore—and so won't mind if you marry someone else."

At the Adler house, an elderly woman stood at the open door, as if waiting for us. "Mr. Sherlock Holmes?" she asked.

"I am he," said Holmes, surprised.

"My mistress said that you'd be here. She left this morning with her husband by the 5:15 train."

"What?" Holmes staggered backward, white with shame and surprise. "She has left England?"

"Never to return."

"All is lost!" cried the king.

"We shall see." Holmes pushed past the woman and rushed to the hiding place. He pulled back the sliding panel, stuck in his hand, and pulled out a photograph and a letter. The photo was of Irene Adler.

The letter was addressed to "Sherlock Holmes." He tore it open, and we three read it together:

Dear Mr. Sherlock Holmes:
    You really did very well. You fooled me completely—until after the fire alarm. But after I'd betrayed my secret place, I began

to think. I was warned of you months ago; I was told that you are a master of disguise. I was sure that the king would hire you, if anyone. It was hard to distrust a kind old clergyman, but disguises are nothing new to me. I am in opera, you'll remember. As soon as you left, I put on my own disguise and followed you. When you stopped at 221-B Baker Street, which I knew is your address, there was no more doubt. My husband and I decided to leave immediately.

You will find the nest empty. As to the photograph and letters, tell the king that he may rest in peace. I love and am loved by a better man than he. But I leave another photo that he may wish to have.

Very truly yours,
Irene Adler Norton

"What a woman!" cried the king of Bohemia. "She is brilliant!"

"Indeed she is," said Holmes coldly. "I am sorry that I could not bring Your Majesty's business to a more successful end."

"On the contrary, dear sir!" said the king. "I know that she won't break her word. I am as safe as if the letters and photo were in the fire."

"I'm glad to hear you say so."

"I am forever in your debt. Will you take money? Jewels? Here, take this ring." He pulled a huge emerald from his finger and held it out to my unhappy friend.

"Your Majesty has something that I would value much more," said Holmes.

"Name it!"

"This photograph."

"Irene's photograph?" asked the king. "Certainly, if you wish it."

"Thank you," said Holmes, still icy. "There is no more to be done. I have the honor of wishing you a very good morning, Your Majesty." He turned and left, without noticing the hand the king held out for him to shake.

That was how a great scandal had

threatened to affect the kingdom of Bohemia—and how the best plans of Sherlock Holmes had been beaten by a woman's wit. To this day, whenever he speaks of Irene Adler or refers to her photograph, it is always under the honorable title of *the* woman.

CASE #4

THE ADVENTURE OF THE BLUE CARBUNCLE

I

The second morning after Christmas, I visited 221-B Baker Street, to wish my friend season's greetings. Holmes was stretched out on the sofa with a pile of just-read newspapers crumpled nearby. A chair had been pulled next to the sofa, and on its back hung a very seedy-looking hat. Holmes's magnifying glass lay on the chair's seat. It appeared that he'd been studying the hat very closely.

"Oh, you're busy," I said. "Sorry to interrupt you."

"No, no, please come in," said Holmes cheerfully.

"That homely-looking hat must have some deadly story tied to it," I said, "and you're looking for clues that will help you solve the crime."

"There's no crime," said Holmes, laughing. "You know Peterson, who works down the street? He found it. That dirty, broken-down hat is an interesting puzzle to be solved. Peterson came here Christmas morning, with the hat and a fine fat goose, which must be roasting at his fire this minute."

"What happened?" I asked.

"Here are the facts: About four o'clock on Christmas morning, Peterson was coming home from a holiday party. Walking just ahead of him on Tottenham Court Road was a tallish man, staggering a little and carrying a white goose over his shoulder. As he reached the corner of Goodge Street, a bunch of ruffians surrounded the man and there was a fuss. One ruffian knocked off the man's hat, and he raised his walking stick to defend himself. He swung it too hard and smashed the shop window behind him. Peterson dashed over to help the man fight off the ruffians, but the man seemed stunned by the smashed window. When he saw a police officer coming, he dropped his goose and took off. The ruffians ran, too, so Peterson was left with this battered hat and a splendid Christmas goose."

"Peterson's an honest fellow," I said with surpirse. "Why didn't he return them to their owner?"

"My dear Watson, that is the problem at hand. There was a tag tied to the goose's leg, with 'FOR MRS. HENRY BAKER' printed on it, and the initials *H.B.* are written inside the hat. But thousands of Bakers, and hundreds of Henry Bakers, live in this city. So Peterson brought the hat and goose to me, knowing how much I enjoy solving problems. I told him to take the goose home to his family and enjoy it, since it would spoil if not cooked and eaten soon. Meanwhile, I've been studying the hat, searching for clues to its owner's identity. I have some ideas. You know my methods, Watson. Have a

look at the hat. What can you deduce about its owner, my friend?"

I took the tattered thing and turned it over in my hands. It was an ordinary black derby of the usual round shape, very much worse for the wear. Its silk lining had been red, but it was now faded and discolored. There was no maker's name but, as Holmes had said, the initials *H. B.* were written on one side. It was cracked, very dusty, and spotted in several places, but someone had tried to hide the stains by smearing them with black ink.

"I see nothing," I said, handing it back to my friend.

"You see everything, Watson. You just aren't using what you see."

"Okay," I challenged. "What do *you* get from what you see?"

"Well," said he, "the man is quite intelligent. He was fairly well-to-do within the last three years, but has fallen upon hard times. He used to be a careful, thoughtful man. He is less so now, suggesting that there may be evil influences on him—perhaps he drinks too much. That may be why his wife has stopped loving him."

"Holmes! How can you—"

"He does, however, have some self-respect left," Holmes continued. "He leads a quiet life, rarely goes out, is completely out of shape, is middle-aged. He has graying hair that's been cut within the last few days, hair on which he uses lime-cream. These are just the more obvious facts to be deduced from this hat."

"I can't see how you know all that. Why do you say he's quite intelligent?"

Holmes set the hat on his own head. It was too big; it came over his forehead and rested on the bridge of his nose. "He has a very large head," said Holmes. "A man with so large a brain must have something in it."

"His change in fortune, then?"

"This hat is of a style that came in three years ago, when it was new. It is of the highest quality—look at the silk band and lining. If he could afford to buy a hat like this three years ago, he was well-off. He hasn't been able to buy one since, however, so it's clear that he's gone down in the world."

"Okay. But the other things—"

"The many recent stains show that he's not as careful as he used to be. Still, he tried to cover them with ink, showing that he has *some* self-respect left. That he's middle-aged and has graying brown hair that's been cut recently and that he uses lime-cream on it? Look at the lining with the magnifying glass! There are lots of very short hairs, part gray and part brown, with sharp, scissor-cut ends. They are sticky, and smell of lime-cream. The dust on this hat isn't street dust, but the fluffy brown sort found inside houses. So it spends more time indoors than on his head outside, which means that he rarely goes out. The inner band shows sweat stains, so the owner perspired a lot, the way someone out of shape is likely to do."

"But his wife, Holmes! How can you say that she's stopped loving him?"

"This hat hasn't been brushed in weeks. A loving wife would never let her husband leave the house with such a wreck on his head. She'd make sure that he looked presentable, even if they didn't have a penny to spare."

"Maybe he's a bachelor."

"He was taking the goose home to 'MRS. HENRY BAKER'—probably as a peace offering."

"You have an answer to everything," I said, laughing. "But since no crime has been committed, all your work seems a waste of energy."

II

Just then, the door flew open and Peterson rushed in. His face was red and his eyes looked dazed with astonishment.

"The goose, Mr. Holmes, the goose!" Peterson gasped.

"What about it?" asked my friend. "Did it suddenly come back to life and fly out the window? Calm yourself!"

"Look, sir, at what my wife found in its throat!"

Peterson held out his hand. There, on his palm, was a brilliant blue gemstone. It was only about the size of a bean, but it was so pure and glowing that it seemed filled with light.

Holmes sat up with a whistle. "By Jove, Peterson, this is quite a treasure. Do you know what you've got?"

"A precious stone?"

"It's not just any precious stone. It's *the* precious stone."

"Not the Countess of Morcar's blue carbuncle!" I exclaimed. "The one that was stolen a few days ago? It's in all the newspapers."

"The very one," said Holmes calmly. "It is absolutely unique. The Countess of

Morcar is offering a reward of £1,000, so its real value must be at least twenty times that."

"A thousand pounds! Oh, mercy!" Peterson had gone pale, and collapsed onto the nearest chair.

"It was stolen from the Hotel Cosmopolitan," I said.

"Correct," said Holmes. "On December 22, just five days ago. A plumber named John Horner was arrested for the crime." Holmes pulled an item from his pile of newspapers. "Here," he said. "Look at this."

HOTEL COSMOPOLITAN
JEWEL ROBBERY
John Horner, 26, plumber, has been charged with stealing the valuable gem known as the blue carbuncle from the room of the Countess of Morcar. James Ryder, an attendant at the hotel, told police that he'd taken Horner to that room on December 22 to make a minor repair.

He was called away for a few minutes, and returned to find Horner gone. A locked drawer had been forced open, and a leather jewel case was empty. Ryder sounded an alarm.

Catherine Cusack, maid to the Countess, told police that she had heard Ryder's yell and rushed into the room. She, too, saw the empty case—the one where the Countess kept her priceless blue carbuncle.

Horner was arrested that evening, but no stone was found on his person or in his home. Inspector Bradstreet, the arresting officer, said that Horner had claimed innocence, insisting that he knew nothing about the jewel. Since Horner has a record for robbery, a judge ordered that he remain in jail until his trial. On hearing this, Horner fainted and had to be carried from the courtroom.

"Hmmm," said Holmes. "So much for the police court. You see, Watson? Our little deductions have suddenly become very important. A crime was committed, after all. What happened between the raiding of a jewel case at the Hotel Cosmopolitan and the dropping of a goose at the corner of Goodge Street? Here is the stone; it came from the goose, which came from Mr. Henry Baker, the gentleman with the wretched hat. We must find that gentleman and see what part he played in this little mystery. We'll try the simplest thing first."

"What's that?" I asked.

"I'll put an ad in the newspapers," he replied, beginning to write. "Here's what I'll say: 'Found at the corner of Goodge Street: A goose and a black felt hat. Mr. Henry Baker can have them by coming, at 6:30 this evening, to 221-B Baker Street.' Here, Peterson, please have this ad put in all the evening newspapers."

"Very well, sir. What about the stone?"

"I'll keep it safe. While you're out,

please buy a goose of the same size as the one you found, and bring it back here. We'll need one to give Mr. Baker."

When Peterson had gone, Holmes picked up the stone and held it up to the light. "It's beautiful, isn't it, Watson? See how it sparkles! Of course it's tied to a crime—every good stone is. I'll lock it in my strongbox and send a message to the Countess, letting her know that it's safe."

"Do you think that man Horner is innocent?" I asked.

"I can't tell."

"How about Henry Baker?"

"I think he had no idea that his bird had a treasure inside it, but I can't say for sure. I'll have proof if he answers my ad. We can't know more till then."

III

At just past 6:30, a tallish man arrived at Holmes's door.

"Mr. Henry Baker, I believe," said Holmes, rising to shake the stranger's hand. "Please, have a seat by the fire— it's a cold night."

Our visitor did so, and we joined him.

"Is that your hat, Mr. Baker?" asked Holmes, pointing to where it still hung on the chair.

"It is indeed my hat," said the man. He had a massive head and a broad, intelligent-looking face. His hair and beard were brown but going gray. His

nose and cheeks were redder than normal and his hands shook a bit— signs of a drinking problem, as Holmes had thought.

"We've had these things for a few days," said Holmes, "expecting to see an ad in the papers, giving your address. Why didn't you advertise?"

Our visitor gave an embarrassed laugh. "I don't have as much money as I used to," he said. "I figured that the thugs had run off with my hat and goose, so it didn't seem worthwhile for me to spend money on an ad."

"That makes sense," said Holmes. "Well, we had to eat the goose."

"Eat it!" cried Baker.

"It was about to spoil," said Holmes. "But will this other goose do? It's about the same size and weight as yours, and it's quite fresh."

"Oh, that would be fine," said Baker, looking relieved.

"We still have the feathers and

innards of your bird, if you'd like to have them—"

The man burst out laughing. "Why would I want *them*? I'll be happy to have just that excellent bird, and my hat."

Holmes shrugged his shoulders. "Very well, then, there they are."

Baker rose and put the hat on his head and the goose under his arm.

"Do you mind if I ask you where your lost goose came from?" said Holmes. "I love a fine cooked bird, and that was one of the best I've ever had."

"A group of my friends started a goose club," said Baker. "Each week, we gave a few pennies to Windigate, host at the Alpha Inn, and he put them away. At the end of the year, there was enough saved for each man to have a Christmas goose. Windigate ordered them and handed them out on Christmas Eve. The rest you know. I thank you, sir, and wish you both a happy new year."

Henry Baker bowed and left us.

"Well, it's clear that *he's* innocent," said Holmes. "Care to join me, Watson? I want to follow up this clue while it's still hot."

IV

We put on our coats and hats and wrapped scarves around our necks, then went out into the bitter night. A quarter-hour's walk took us to the Alpha Inn. We entered, and Holmes approached the white-aproned landlord.

"If your food is as excellent as your Christmas geese," said Holmes, "I'm sure that this is a fine establishment."

"My geese!" The man stared at him, looking surprised.

"Yes," said Holmes. "I was just talking with Henry Baker, a member of your goose club."

"Oh, I see," said Windigate. "But those aren't *my* geese."

"No? Where did you get them, then?"

"I bought the two dozen from a salesman in Covent Garden."

"I know those shops," said Holmes. "Which one was it?"

"A fellow named Breckinridge."

"Don't know him," said Holmes. "Ah, well. Thanks anyway, sir. Good night and good luck to you."

Once more, we strode through the night, this time heading for the Covent Garden markets.

"Remember, Watson," warned my friend, "we may be getting closer to a

desperate man who has risked life and limb to steal a priceless jewel, then lost it. There's another man to remember, too—a man now in jail, facing seven years' hard time unless we can prove his innocence."

At Covent Garden, we saw a sign saying BRECKINRIDGE above one of the larger stalls. A horsey-looking man and a boy were shutting up for the night.

"Good evening to you," said Holmes. "Sold out of geese, I see."

The man gave him a sharp look. "Let you have five hundred in the morning."

"That's no help," said Holmes.

"Well, try the shop next door," said the salesman.

"Ah, but I was recommended to you," said my friend.

"Really? Who by?"

"The innkeeper at the Alpha."

"Oh, yes. I sent him two dozen geese just before Christmas."

"Fine birds they were, too," said Holmes. "Where were they from?"

To my surprise, the salesman suddenly lost his temper.

"Now see here," he demanded. "What are you getting at? I sell a good product, and that should be an end to it. But now, all of a sudden, I've got people coming round wanting to know, 'Where are the geese?' and 'Who did you sell them to?' and now it's 'Where did you get them?' You'd think they were the only geese in the world!"

"I have nothing to do with anyone else asking about your geese," said Holmes mildly. "I'm only trying to settle a bet. I bet my friend here a fiver that the goose I ate from the Alpha was country bred."

"Well, you've lost your fiver," snapped the salesman. "It was city bred."

"It couldn't be!" argued Holmes.

"It was."

"Wasn't! Bet you a tenner it wasn't."

"Was, too," said the man. "It'll be easy taking your money. I can prove it. You, Bill!" he said to the boy. "Bring me the record book."

The boy brought him a huge book, which he lay near the lamp.

"Now, then, Mr. Know-It-All," the man told Holmes, "look right here. This book is where I list the names and addresses of everyone I buy from and all my orders. The country folk are listed on this side, the city folk on the other. Take a look at the third name on the city side."

"Mrs. Oakshott, 117 Brixton Road," read Holmes.

"Now check the orders list. What do you see there?"

Holmes found it. "It says, 'Mrs. Oakshott, egg and poultry supplier.' "

"And the last entry there?"

"December 22: Twenty-four geese at seven shillings, sixpence. Sold to Mr. Windigate, Alpha Inn."

The salesman laughed at Holmes's disappointed-looking face. "Yes, sir. The last time I looked, 117 Brixton Road was in the city. You've lost your bet. Let's have that tenner!"

Holmes threw down the money as if disgusted, and we left. Once around the corner, however, he stopped and burst out laughing. "I could tell the moment I spotted that fellow that he liked a good bet. I knew I'd get more information by betting him a ten than by trying to bribe him with a hundred!"

V

As we stood there, a sudden hubbub broke out at the shop we'd just left. We turned back to see Breckinridge, the salesman, shaking his fist at a little rat-faced man.

"I've had enough of you and your geese!" shouted Breckinridge. "Get out of here at once!"

"But one of those geese was mine," whined the little man.

"Then ask Mrs. Oakshott about it!"

"I did, and she told me to ask you."

"You can ask the king of Prussia, for all I care," shouted Breckinridge, "but don't bother me a minute more!" He rushed fiercely at the little man, who turned and ran.

"Excellent!" said Holmes with delight. "This may save us a trip to Brixton Road. Come on, Watson!" We took off after the rat-faced man.

Holmes soon caught up with him and tapped his shoulder. The man sprang around, looking pale and frightened. "What do you want?" he asked.

"Pardon me," said Holmes, "but I couldn't help overhearing your argument. I believe I can help you."

"Who are you?" cried the man. "What do *you* know of this?"

"My name is Sherlock Holmes," came the reply, "and it's my business to know things that other people don't."

"Well, you don't know about this."

"I know everything about it," said Holmes. "You're looking for two dozen geese that Mrs. Oakshott of Brixton Road sold to a shopkeeper named Breckinridge, who sold them to Mr. Windigate of the Alpha Inn, who bought them for his club."

"Oh, sir, you're just the man I'd hoped to meet!" said the little man. "I can't tell you how important this is to me."

"In that case," said Holmes, hailing a cab, "let's get out of this cold, windy street and talk someplace cozier. But first, tell me: What is your name?"

The man hesitated a moment. "John Robinson," he said.

"No, no, your *real* name," said Holmes sweetly.

The man blushed and stammered. "Well, then, it's—er, well—my real name is James Ryder."

"Exactly so," said Holmes. "Head attendant at the Cosmopolitan Hotel."

The little man looked from Holmes to me and back again, half-hopeful and half-suspicious. Then he shrugged and got into the cab. Soon we three were at Baker Street, sitting by the fire.

"Now," said Holmes. "You want to know what became of all those geese. Or, to be exact, one goose—white, with a black bar across its tail."

The little man shook with emotion. "That's the one! What became of it?"

"It came here. A remarkable bird it was, too: It laid an egg after it was dead! The prettiest, brightest little blue egg you ever did see. I have it right here." Holmes unlocked his strongbox and took out the blue carbuncle. Ryder staggered to his feet in shock.

"The game is up, Ryder," said Holmes. "You're going to prison. I have all the proof I need, but you can fill in a detail or two. How did you learn about this blue stone of the Countess of Morcar?"

"Catherine Cusack told me about it," said Ryder in a broken voice.

"Ah, yes. The Countess's maid. Fine jewels have tempted better men than you, Ryder, but you did more than just steal it. You knew of Horner's past, so you set him up to take the blame for *your* crime!"

Ryder threw himself to the floor and shamelessly clutched my friend's knees. "Please, please," he wailed. "Have mercy! Think of my father! Think of my mother! This will break their hearts! I'll never do wrong again! I swear!"

"You should have thought of your parents' hearts before committing your crimes," Holmes said coldly. "How did the stone end up inside the goose?"

"Maggie Oakshott is my sister," whined the miserable man. "I had to hide the stone quickly, in case the police searched me or my home. Maggie and her husband had promised me one of their geese for Christmas. The police would never think

to look inside a goose! So I went to the Oakshotts', found a goose different from the others, and jammed the stone down its throat. The bird made such a racket that Maggie came out to see what was going on. I was so startled that I let go, and the goose flapped off to join the others.

" 'What were you doing to that bird?' she wanted to know.

" 'Oh, I was just trying to see which one is fattest. You said I could have one, don't you remember?'

"She said that they'd already set one aside for me, an extra fat one, but I told her I wanted the one that *I'd* picked. She said I could take whichever bird I wanted. I found the one with the barred tail, killed it, and took it with me. But when I took the goose to the man who was going to buy the stone, we cut it open and nothing was there! I ran back to my sister's in a panic, but all the birds were gone. She said that she'd kept one for her family and sold the other 24 to Breckinridge, of

Covent Garden. I asked if any of them had a barred tail and she said yes, two, and she never could tell them apart. I'd taken one, and the other had gone to Breckinridge! I ran there at once, but it was too late and—well, you gentlemen know the rest. My sister thinks that I've gone crazy, and maybe I have. I ruined myself! I sold my soul for a fortune I'll never even have. Oh, please have mercy!"

The wretch buried his face in his hands and wept. There was a long silence, broken only by the man's pitiful sobs and the tapping of Holmes's fingers on the tabletop. Finally, my friend stood up, crossed the room, and flung open the door.

"Get out!" he ordered.

Ryder blinked in amazement. "Yes, sir! Thank you, sir!" In a trice he had

flown out the door, down the stairs, onto the street, and away.

"You look surprised, Watson," said Holmes. "The police haven't hired me to make up for their mistakes. If Horner were in danger of being convicted, it would be different. But the only man who could testify against him is Ryder, and you can be sure that *he* won't dare show his face in court! The case will collapse and Horner will be freed."

"But Holmes—"

"Ryder won't go wrong again—he's too frightened. Besides, isn't Christmas the season of forgiveness? Now, my good friend, would you ring the bell for the maid? I think I'm ready to begin a new investigation—of my dinner!"

The Adventure of the Engineer's Thumb

I

Of all the great cases Sherlock Holmes had during our friendship, only two were brought to his attention by me. The case of Mr. Hatherly's thumb is one of them.

It was in the summer of 1889, not long after I got married and returned to practicing medicine. One of my patients was a guard at the nearby railroad station. I had cured him of a long, painful illness, and he was grateful. After that, he sent every sufferer he knew to my office. One morning, a little before seven o'clock, the maid woke me. The railroad guard had come, she said, with someone in need of my medical skills. I dressed and hurried downstairs.

"I have a patient for you, Doctor," said the guard. "He seems to be all right, but I think he's in shock. I was afraid he might wander off, so I brought him here myself. Now that he's in good hands, I'll get back to my job."

A young gentleman, no older than 25, was waiting in my treatment room. A bloodstained handkerchief was wrapped around one of his hands and his face was very pale. He looked as if he were struggling to control some great emotion.

"I'm sorry to get you up so early, Doctor," he said, "but I had a serious accident during the night. I arrived by train this morning, and asked at the station where I could find a doctor. My name is Victor Hatherly."

"I'm sorry I kept you waiting," I said. "An overnight train ride can be quite dull enough, I know."

"Oh, I'd hardly call my night dull!" he said, and laughed. He laughed harder and harder, with a high ringing note. I recognized it as the hysteria that sometimes comes over a person who has come through a great crisis.

"Pull yourself together!" I snapped.

But he laughed until it wore him out. Then he gazed at me with weary eyes. "I'm sorry," he said.

"That's all right. Drink this." I gave him some water. He drank it down.

"Thank you, Doctor," he said. "That's better. Now, perhaps you should take care of my thumb—or at least the place where my thumb used to be."

He unwrapped the handkerchief and held out his hand. Even with all my experience as a wartime army doctor, the sight made me shudder. There, next to his four fingers, was a horrid red spot where a thumb should have been. It had been hacked right off.

"Good heavens!" I cried. "What a terrible injury! It must have bled a lot."

"Yes," said he. "I fainted. When I came to, I wrapped it as tightly as I could and it seemed to help."

"You did a very good job," I told him as I examined his wound. "This was done with a very sharp and heavy instrument."

"A cleaver," he said.

"Was it an accident?" I asked.

"Absolutely not," he replied.

"A murderous attack?"

"Very murderous indeed," he said.

I cleaned and treated the wound, then wrapped it in bandages.

"That's much better, thank you," he said. "Now I must go tell my tale to the police. It's such as strange story, though, that if it weren't for this wound of mine I doubt that they'd believe me. I couldn't blame them. I haven't a shred of proof, and no way to find the villain who did this."

"If you need a problem solved, you should see my friend Sherlock Holmes," I told him.

"Sherlock Holmes? I've heard of that fellow," said my patient. "I'd be very happy if he'd take my case. Will you introduce me to him?"

"Of course!" I said. "We'll call a cab and go to him at once."

II

When we reached Baker Street, Holmes was about to sit down to a hearty breakfast, and insisted that we join him. Afterward, he settled Hatherly on the sofa, with a pillow beneath his head.

"Now," said Holmes, "tell us what you can." Holmes sat back in his big armchair and gazed at Hatherly with his eyes half-closed, the way he always did when he listened intently.

"I am a hydraulic engineer," said Hatherly. "A very good one. Two years ago, I left the engineering firm where I'd learned my trade and went into business for myself. It has been hard going, I'm afraid. Despite all my skills, it hasn't been easy attracting new clients to my little third-floor office. Every day, from nine in the morning till four in the afternoon, I wait there, hoping for someone to walk in and hire me. I've had only four small jobs in two years.

"Yesterday, a gentleman came in. He handed me his business card: 'Colonel Lysander Stark,' it said. He was taller than average, balding, and I've never seen anyone so thin. His whole face was

sharpened away into nose and chin, and his cheekbones almost stuck out of his skin. He was plainly and neatly dressed, and his age was close to forty. He spoke with a slight German accent.

" 'Mr. Hatherly,' he said, 'I need the services of a hydraulic engineer, and you have been highly recommended to me. I have been told that you're not only skilled at your job, but you're also a man who can be trusted to keep a secret.'

"I was flattered, and asked who had recommended me to him, but he waved the question aside. He did say, however, that he'd also been told that I'm an orphan and a bachelor, and live alone in London.

" 'That's true,' I told him. 'But what has that to do with my professional skills? Aren't you here to discuss a professional matter?'

" 'Yes,' he said, 'I wish to hire you. But you must understand that absolute secrecy is called for—*absolute* secrecy! A man who lives alone should find it easier to keep a secret than a man who is surrounded by family.'

" 'If I promise to keep a secret, I keep it,' I said.

"He was staring suspiciously at me. 'Do you promise?' he asked.

" 'I promise,' I said.

" 'Absolute and complete silence before, during, and after the job? You'll never speak or write to anyone about any of it?'

" 'I've already given you my word, sir.'

"'Good!' He suddenly stood up, darted across the floor, and threw open the office door. He stared up and down the hallway, making sure it was empty, then shut the door and came back. 'Now,' he said, 'we may talk in safety.'

"His strange behavior was making me nervous—as well as impatient. 'Could we get down to business, sir?' I said. 'My time is valuable!' Heaven help me for saying those words! The man then offered me

fifty guineas for one night's work. That is ten times what I would have said if he'd asked what my fee would be!

" 'I say a night's work,' said the Colonel, 'but an hour would be nearer the truth. I just need you to look at a stamping machine that seems to have slipped out of gear. We'd want you to come out tonight by the last train.'

" 'Where to?'

" 'To Eyford, a little place about seven miles from Reading. There's a train leaving London that would get you there about 11:15. I'll come down in a carriage to meet you,' he replied.

" 'Is it a long drive from there?' I asked.

" 'Oh, yes, our place is way out in the country. It'll be midnight before we reach it. You'd miss the last train back, but we can put you up for the night.'

" 'Couldn't I come at a more convenient hour?' I suggested.

" 'We are paying you very well for very little work," the Colonel snapped, "and you have no family to rush back to. But if you don't want the job—'

"I told him that I *did* want it, of course, and asked him for more details about the job. His story was vague and rather strange—something about having discovered a valuable ore in his backyard, and wanting to mine as much as possible without his neighbors noticing. He

would sell that ore, then use the money to buy his neighbors' land before they realized how much it was worth. He wanted me to come in the middle of the night, because if the neighbors heard that a hydraulic engineer had come, they might get suspicious and ruin all his plans.

"His story didn't make much sense to me. What good is a stamping machine in digging ore? When I asked him that, he said that he and a partner had come up with their own secret process for pressing the ore into bricks.

"He finally left, after reminding me of what train I should take and making me swear, yet again, that I'd keep his secret.

"When I look back now, I see so many warning signs that I should have heeded. The huge fee should have been a warning—it was far too much for what he said he wanted done. That fee is what drowned my good sense!"

III

Hatherly took a deep breath, then continued his tale.

"I followed the Colonel's instructions exactly," he said, "and arrived at Eyford just after eleven o'clock. It's a little, dimly lit station, and I was the only passenger who got off there. The Colonel was there, waiting in the shadows with a carriage. He grabbed my arm and hustled me inside. The moment we were inside, he tapped on the roof to signal the driver, and we took off as fast as the horse could go.

"One horse?" asked Holmes.

"Yes, only one."

"Tired-looking or fresh?"

"Oh, quite fresh and glossy."

"Thank you," said Holmes. "Please, continue with your story."

"We drove for at least an hour. The Colonel had said that it was about a seven-mile trip, but it seemed closer to

twelve. He never said a word, but whenever I looked his way, he was staring at me with great intensity. The windows were of frosted glass, so I couldn't see anything. We rocked and lurched so much that we must have been on bad country roads. Finally, the carriage turned onto a smooth gravel drive and stopped. The Colonel got out first and, as soon as I stepped out, he grabbed my arm and pulled me into a house before I could look around. I heard the carriage roll away, then all was silence.

"It was pitch dark inside the house. While the Colonel was fumbling for candles, a door opened at the other end of the hall. A woman stood there, holding a lamp above her head, trying to see us. She asked a question in a foreign language and the Colonel snapped back an answer that startled her so much she nearly dropped her lamp. He went over to her, took her lamp, and pushed her back into the room and shut the door. He led me to another room, set down the lamp, and asked me to wait there. He left, closing the door behind him.

"There was a piano in the room, and lots of books written in German. I went to the window, hoping to catch a glimpse of the countryside, but the shutters were closed and locked tight. Except for a clock ticking in the hallway, the house was deathly quiet. I couldn't help but feel uneasy.

"Suddenly, the door swung open and the woman came in. Her beautiful face looked frightened, but she spoke calmly to me in broken English.

" 'I would go,' she said. 'Please, I would go. I should not stay here. There is no good for you to do.'

" 'But I haven't done what I've been hired to do,' I told her.

" 'No, better to go. Door is open.' When I smiled and shook my head, she suddenly gave up trying to seem calm. 'Please!' she whispered desperately. 'For the love of Heaven, get away from here before it's too late!'

"I'd had a long, wearisome journey, and hadn't been paid yet. Besides, for all I knew, this lady might be a madwoman, kept locked in the house. So I shook my head no again.

"She was about to argue further when we heard footsteps on the stairs. In a flash, she was gone.

"Moments later, Colonel Stark appeared with another man—a short, thick fellow with a furry-looking beard. The Colonel introduced him as Mr. Ferguson, his secretary and manager.

"The Colonel gave me a suspicious look. 'I remember closing this door when I left you,' he said.

" 'It seemed a little stuffy in here,' I said. 'So I opened it.'

"He gave me another suspicious look, but all he said was, 'Come. I'll take you to the machine.' I reached for my hat, but he said to leave it—the machine was upstairs! I was amazed, for who would have a mining machine inside a house? The two men took me upstairs and the Colonel led me inside. It was a square room, so small that Ferguson had to wait outside.

" 'We are now inside the hydraulic press,' said the Colonel. 'That isn't a ceiling above our heads, but a metal plate. It comes down onto this metal floor with the force of many tons. The machine doesn't work as well as it used to. Can you figure out why and fix it?'

"I looked the machine over and soon spotted the problem. It was easy to fix, and I showed him how. However, my examination told me something else: His story about using the press in mining ore was a lie. The machine was far too powerful for that sort of work. Besides, there wasn't a speck of dirt on the metal floor! My lamp caught glints of something else, though—tiny bits of silvery metal! Suddenly, the Colonel loomed over me.

" 'What are you doing there?' he growled.

"I was so angry at being tricked that I didn't think before I spoke. 'If you would just tell me what you *really* use this machine for, I could do a better job of helping you fix it!'

"The moment I said it, I was sorry. His face suddenly turned cruel. 'Very well,' he said. 'I'll give you a fine chance to see how it works!' He stepped backward and out the door, slamming it behind him and locking it tight! I dashed over to it, and tugged at the handle. I was trapped! I kicked, pushed, and yelled. But the only

other sound I could hear made my blood run cold: The clanking of levers and chains. He had turned on the machine!

"I threw myself against the door, scraping my fingers bloody and screaming for mercy. The heavy press kept clanking closer with terrifying speed. I knew that I'd be crushed flat in seconds. I crouched in terror—then noticed a sliver of yellow light between two boards in the wall. I threw myself against it—and crashed through just seconds before the terrible press would have crushed out my life!

"As I lay there gasping for breath, the beautiful woman appeared at my side. She tugged my sleeve and cried, 'Come quickly! Once they realize you aren't in there, they'll come looking for you!'

"We ran. She led me to a window and threw it open. 'Is high,' she said, 'but you must jump. If they catch you, they will kill you!'

"I climbed out just as the Colonel flew in, rage twisting his face. The woman tried to hold him back. 'Fritz! Fritz!' she cried in English, 'you promised me! No more killing after that other one!'

"I should have jumped and been gone, but I wanted to be sure that the villain didn't hurt her for helping me. I hung there, ready to climb back in to defend her if he did.

" 'You'll ruin us, Elise! He has seen too much!' Before I realized what was happening, he shoved her aside and ran to the window, cutting at me with his heavy weapon. I felt a dull pain, let go, and fell crashing into the garden. I heard him yelling as I got up and ran as hard as I could. But I hadn't gotten far before I felt so dizzy, I was afraid that I would faint. That's when I looked down and saw that my thumb was missing! I pulled out my handkerchief and tied it tightly over the wound. Then I heard a buzz in my ears, and crashed into the rosebushes in a dead faint.

"When I fell from the window it was a dark night with a bright moon. When I came to, the sky was bright with dawn. Stranger than that was what I saw when I looked around. Instead of a house, and a garden with rosebushes, I was lying near a main road. And there, just a few yards away, was the Eyford train station, where I'd arrived the night before! How I had traveled ten or twelve miles without knowing it—without even

knowing which direction to travel in— I couldn't imagine!

"I stumbled to the station. I asked the stationmaster if he had ever heard of Colonel Lysander Stark and he said no. I asked where the nearest police station was, but it was three miles away. I had no way to get there, though, and the train to London was coming, so I took that. You gentlemen know the rest."

Holmes and I sat in silence for a little while. What an amazing story! Then Holmes stood up and pulled out his collection of crime stories clipped from newspapers. "This will interest you," he told us. "It was in all the papers about a year ago. Listen to this:

Lost, on the 9th of this month, Mr. Jeremiah Hayling, aged 26, a hydraulic engineer. Left his home at ten o'clock that night, and has not been heard of since. Was dressed in—

"And so on. So! That must have been the last time the Colonel's machine needed fixing."

"Good heavens!" cried Hatherly. "That explains what the woman said about 'that other one.' "

"Yes," said Holmes. "This colonel is obviously a desperate man who would rather kill than allow his little game to be uncovered. We mustn't waste another moment! Let's get the police and go to Eyford at once."

IV

Three hours later, a group of five was on the train to Eyford: Sherlock Holmes, the engineer, Police Inspector Bradstreet, a plainclothes police officer, and myself. The inspector was studying a map of the Eyford area. He drew a circle with Eyford at its center, the line marking ten miles' distance from that town.

"You said an hour's drive," said Bradstreet to Hatherly. "That gives us quite a large area to cover. I wish we knew in which direction to start looking."

"I can lay my finger on it," said Holmes quietly.

"Nonsense, Holmes," said Bradstreet. "It could be any direction! I say south—that area seems more deserted."

"I say east," said Hatherly.

"I say west," said the plainclothes officer. "There are a few little villages there."

"I say north," I said. "There are no hills there and our friend didn't notice the carriage going up or down."

"You're all wrong," said Holmes, pointing to the map. "This is where we shall find them." His fingertip was right in the middle of the circle—on Eyford itself!

"But the twelve-mile drive!" gasped a confused Hatherly.

"Six out," said Holmes, "and six back. They did it to confuse you. You said that the horse was fresh and glossy when you got in the carriage. It couldn't have been if it had just come twelve miles to fetch you."

"This is a very sneaky gang," said the inspector with a smile.

"Yes," said Holmes. "It's clear what they

were up to: using that press to pound together the metals used to make coins."

"Counterfeiters!" I exclaimed.

"We've been trying to find a clever gang of counterfeiters for some time now," said the inspector. "They've been making fake coins by the thousands! Now I'll finally get my hands on them!"

But the inspector never got that chance. As our train rolled into Eyford, we saw a huge cloud of smoke rising from behind a clump of nearby trees.

"A house on fire?" asked Bradstreet.

"Yes," said the stationmaster. "It

broke out during the night, but by the time anyone noticed it, the flames had spread beyond control."

"Whose house is it?"

"Dr. Becher's."

"Is he German," asked Hatherly, "very thin, with a long, sharp nose?"

"Not at all!" said the stationmaster with a laugh. "Quite the opposite—a very short and very round Englishman. But he has a friend staying with him who's quite on the narrow side!"

We hurried toward the burning house. Flames shot out of every door and window, while three fire engines pumped out water that seemed to do no good.

"That's the place!" cried Hatherly. "There's the gravel drive, and the front door, and the rosebushes where I collapsed! And that window up there, that's the one I fell from."

"Well," said Holmes, "at least you've had some revenge on them. Their precious machine and their evil business have

been ruined. Your oil lamp, which was left in the press when you escaped, started the fire when it was crushed. The wooden walls caught fire, but the men were too busy chasing you to notice until it was too late. Search the crowd for their faces, but I'm sure that they're long gone by now."

Holmes was right, as usual. No word has ever been heard of the beautiful woman, the sinister Colonel, or his chubby friend. Not even Holmes, with all his amazing skills, was ever able to turn up a clue to where they'd gone.

"Well," said the young engineer as we rode the train back to London. "This has been quite some business for me. I've lost my thumb and lost a fifty-guinea fee, and what have I gained?"

"Experience," said Holmes with a smile. "And, for the rest of your life, you'll have an amazing adventure story that people will beg you to tell!"

—THE END—

ABOUT THE AUTHOR

Sir Arthur Conan Doyle was born in Edinburgh, Scotland, in 1859. Although he became a doctor after graduating from school, Doyle eventually proved to be more successful at writing literature than practicing medicine. His first Sherlock Holmes story, "A Study in Scarlet," was written in 1886. In 1891, Doyle gave up his medical practice to become a full-time author.

Doyle's Sherlock Holmes stories were extremely successful. Fearing that he might become known only for his Holmes tales, Doyle killed off the popular sleuth in an 1893 story. His readers, however, were disappointed by his decision. In 1903, Doyle brought back the character of Sherlock Holmes by popular demand. Doyle continued to write about Holmes until his death in 1930. Today, stories about Holmes continue to be read throughout the world.

Treasury of Illustrated Classics™